Long Johns for a Small Chicken

Long Johns for
A Small Chicken

Written by Esther Silverstein Blanc and Godeane Eagle

Illustrations by Tennessee Dixon

VOLCANO
· PRESS ·

Volcano, California

This publication was made possible through a grant to Women and Children's Support Resources by Paul Blanc, son of Esther Silverstein Blanc (ז״ל), and nephew of Godeane Eagle.

Published by:
Volcano Press
P.O. Box 270, Volcano, California 95689-0270
www.volcanopress.com

Long Johns for a Small Chicken

Library of Congress Cataloging-in-Publication Data

Blanc, Esther Silverstein, 1913–1997
  Long johns for a small chicken / by Esther Silverstein Blanc and Godeane Eagle ; illustrated by Tennessee Dixon.
    p. cm.
  Summary: When a terrible storm blows the feathers off a chick on a western Nebraska farm, a pioneer woman makes clothing from an old pair of long johns to protect him, allowing the chick to grow into a fine rooster.
  ISBN 1-884244-23-8
  [1. Chickens—Fiction. 2. Jews—Nebraska—Fiction. 3. Frontier and pioneer life—Nebraska—Fiction. 4. Nebraska—History—19th century—Fiction.] I. Eagle, Godeane. II. Dixon, Tennessee, ill. III. Title.
PZ7.B586Lo 2003
[Fic]—dc21
                                          2002192812

Special thanks to Ruth I. Gordon, librarian emerita and Joanna McKenna, Volcano Press.

Book layout and typography by Christine Nolt, Cirrus Design, Santa Barbara, California

Book production coordinated by Penelope C. Paine, Santa Barbara, California

Printed in China

10 9 8 7 6 5 4 3 2 1

This book is dedicated to the memory of

Esther Miriam Silverstein Blanc (1913–1997),

truly a woman of valor.

Spring began early that year and lasted a long time. In our town in western Nebraska, Mama's garden was well advanced by the time school was out for the summer.

The day of the storm, Mama had made noodles and was cooking stew for lunch. We took the vegetable basket to the garden, picked early peas, pulled up some baby carrots, and gathered leaf lettuce for a salad.

Mama's chickens, both large and small, were ambling about the chicken yard. The yellow rose bush at the fence had many blooms, and we walked over to admire and smell them.

Although the sun was shining down on us and the air was warm, Mama voiced her uneasiness.

"I think," she said, "that we are going to have a change in the weather."

"What kind of change?" I asked.

"A bad one," Mama replied, shaking her head.

"How can you tell?" I wanted to know.

"After living here for so many years, I can tell." She looked at the sky and listened. "The birds are quiet, the sky has a brassy look and the air feels heavy," she said.

We went into the kitchen through the back porch. We shelled the peas, scraped the carrots, put some potatoes into the stew, and made the salad. Papa came home from the tailor shop and we were ready. The table was set; the stew was on the back of the stove, keeping hot.

While Papa was washing his hands, Mama chased the chickens into the chicken yard. She made sure the door to the chicken coop was open so they could go inside if the rain came.

By the time we finished lunch and Papa had returned to work, the sky had darkened and the air was still—too still! Suddenly, the wind began to blow and the cottonwood trees at the bottom of the garden whipped in wild motion. There was a growing menace in the storm. Lightning flashed, and the thunder that followed seemed closer. Rumbling sounds surrounded us.

Mama looked out the screen door, and saw that one of the chicks was caught on the wire mesh fence of the chicken yard. The little chick hung from the wire by his wing tip, and was being pelted by hail.

Mama dashed into the kitchen, picked up the noodle board, placed it over her head and raced to the fence. Hail in large, round balls pelted down. She freed the battered little bird, and clutching him to her breast, she carried him into the house out of the storm.

I took the noodle board from her as she wrapped the victim of the storm in a clean dishtowel, and placed him gently in the vegetable basket.

We built up the fire in the kitchen stove, warmed a bath towel in the heat of the oven, and looked at the forlorn little chicken. Aside from his wing tips, he was naked to the world. His feathers had been blown away by the storm. Gently, Mama wrapped him in the warm towel. She ran her finger along his small bare neck. "Armes Heltzel," she murmured in Yiddish, "poor little neck." "Heltzel" means "little neck" in Yiddish, and so that is the name we gave our patient.

As soon as another towel was warm, we unwrapped him for a moment. His bruised body felt cold to the touch. He was very still. In time, and after a series of wrappings and unwrappings of heated towels, we heard a faint cheep, and noticed a movement in the basket. We unwrapped him, and our small chicken stood on his feet.

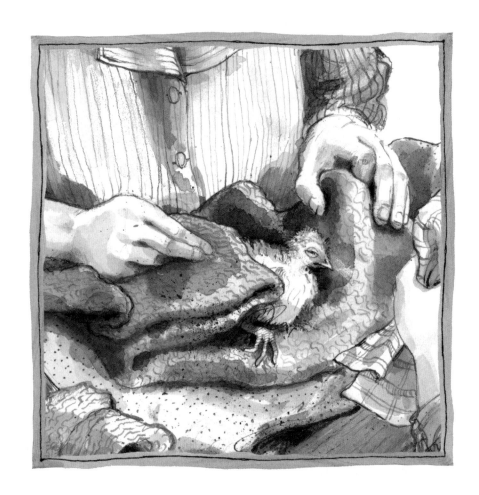

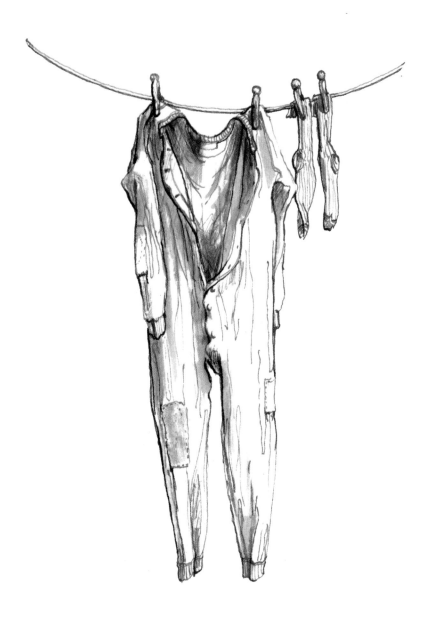

"What he needs," said Mama, "is something to keep him warm and to protect him until his feathers grow in," and so she made a "something" from an old pair of Papa's long johns. She cut a piece from the top, which had both the buttons and the buttonholes, and began to snip and sew and try on.

Soon Heltzel was wearing serviceable long johns, which fitted him loosely. His feet and legs were free, as were his wing tips, where a few feathers still grew. His long johns were open at the bottom so that Heltzel could go to the toilet without soiling his new clothes.

When Papa came home, he reported that the hail had done a great deal of damage. Leaves were stripped from trees, gardens would have to be replanted, and many windows were broken.

I told Papa about Heltzel's rescue and Mama's quick action, and how she had run out holding the noodle board over her head to protect herself from the heavy hailstones. Papa gave me his complete attention. He patted Mama and gave us each a hug.

Mama put clean rags in the basket and made a bed for Heltzel. She placed a small glass of water and a bowl of mashed egg yolk nearby. It was funny to see Heltzel walking about the kitchen floor in his long johns.

After placing him in his basket, we all sat down to supper.

"Papa," I asked, "do you think the long johns are a bit too large for Heltzel?"

"For now," said Papa, "but he will grow into it." The idea of the underwear on the small chicken gave Papa pleasure. "I have been a tailor for forty years," he laughed, "but I never made anything for a small chicken!"

We kept Heltzel in the kitchen for the next few days. "I'm a little worried about him," said Mama. "He has to be returned to the flock quickly, because if he becomes a stranger, the other chickens will peck him."

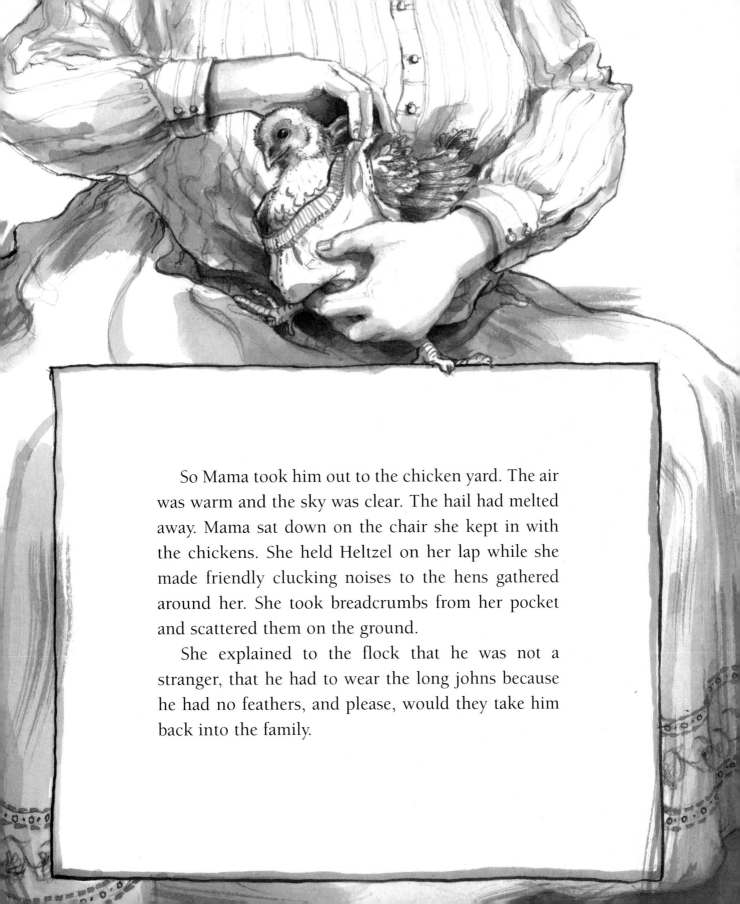

So Mama took him out to the chicken yard. The air was warm and the sky was clear. The hail had melted away. Mama sat down on the chair she kept in with the chickens. She held Heltzel on her lap while she made friendly clucking noises to the hens gathered around her. She took breadcrumbs from her pocket and scattered them on the ground.

She explained to the flock that he was not a stranger, that he had to wear the long johns because he had no feathers, and please, would they take him back into the family.

The hens circled around Mama and seemed to be listening carefully. They cocked their heads from one side to another and shut their eyes one at a time, as if they were thinking over Mama's words.

Mama put Heltzel down on the ground. He began to walk about while Mama scattered more bread-crumbs. The flock accepted Heltzel without incident. With a smile, Mama rose from her chair, shook her apron, and went into the house.

As the weeks passed, Heltzel grew into his long johns. They eventually became a bit tight, so one day in midsummer, Mama unbuttoned him and cut him free. He had grown some feathers and looked almost like the other young chickens that had hatched early in the spring.

By autumn, Heltzel had small spurs on his feet, a
red comb on his head, red feathers and a fine tail.
When he was a year old, he was on his way up in the
chicken society of our flock. We heard his powerful,
clear crow every morning.

I asked Mama, "What will happen to Heltzel?" I needed to know.

"What should happen!" Mama replied. "Do you think I will put him in the soup? When you have saved a life, you can't take it away. Heltzel may live as long as he can, and when he dies, I will bury him under the yellow rose bush by the chicken yard."

Heltzel thrived, and became chief of the chicken yard. He was a large rooster, and we were proud of him, especially Mama.

Papa said, "Even a chicken, to be a success, must have a good mother."

About the Author

Esther Silverstein Blanc was born in 1913, on a homestead in Wyoming. Her parents had moved west to settle on 160 acres of unbroken prairie where they built their dry sod house. Later, the family moved to Mitchell, Nebraska, where Esther graduated from high school, and in 1934, moved to San Francisco to become a registered nurse. Her nursing experiences include a year in a front-line operating room during the Spanish Civil War, and during World War II where she served as a second lieutenant in the U.S. Army Nurse Corps. These experiences she relates in *Wars I Have Seen*, published by Volcano Press. In 1972 she obtained a Ph.D. in the history of medicine, which she taught at the University of California, San Francisco for many years, and retired in 1984. Godeane Eagle is Esther Blanc's sister, and contributed her memories to the story.

About the Illustrator

Says Tennessee Dixon, "I've a long standing affinity with the Great Plains region, from the vast grasslands to the Black Hills. *Long Johns for a Small Chicken* is the second story of Esther's that I've illustrated. As a model for Heltzel, I brought home a chick from the feed store. I reenacted the scenes in the story, including sewing a little cotton outfit as I imagined what Mama would have made for him. The chick went to live on a nice farm. I live in New York City, and sometimes in Hungary, where my son's grandparents live. I make interactive and animated works for multimedia and theater performances."